MW00950677

TINY TRAVELER TALES

Delphine's Surprise

Written by

Rita Tarnate

Illustrated by

Leah Roides

Published by Tiny Traveler Tales
For orders, please visit www.hellozazu.com

Cover design and illustrations by Leah Roides
Hardback ISBN-13: 978-1-7365634-0-3
Paperback ISBN-13: 978-1-7365634-1-0
eBook ISBN-13: 978-1-7365634-2-7

Library of Congress Control Number: 2021904093

To Alex, Odie, Charlie, and Winter. Thank you for your endless support and inspiration. –RMT

To Augusta, Wyatt, and Zion for always creating that spark in my life. For Rita, thank you for asking me to be a part of this amazing journey. –LMR

Meet Delphine. She lives in France with her maman, papa, and her chien, Elodie.

Delphine likes to play and read books.

But, her favorite thing to do is dance.

“Bonjour, Maman!”

“Bonjour, Delphine! It’s time to get dressed,” says Maman. “Papa and I have a surprise for you.”

Vêtements (vet-mahn)

Clothes

Barette (ba-ret)

hair clip

Culotte (koo-lot)

underwear

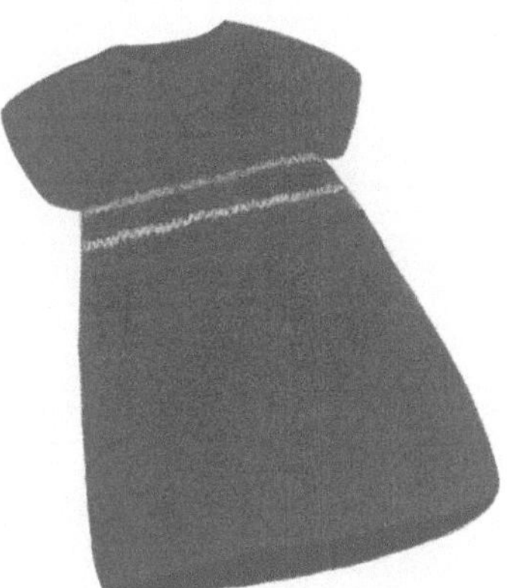

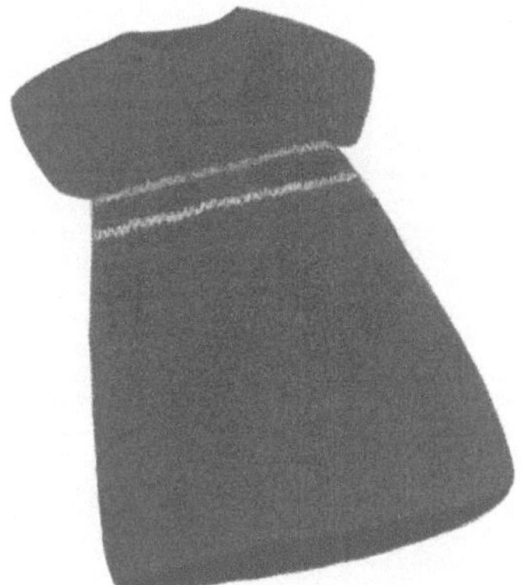

Robe (rob)

dress

Chaussettes (shaw-set)

socks

Chaussures (shaw-soor)

shoes

"Bonjour, Papa! I'm ready for my surprise!"

Papa is making breakfast.

"Bonjour, Delphine! Patience," he laughs.

“First, petit déjeuner,” says Papa.

Petit Déjeuner (puh-tee deh-zhuh-nay)

Breakfast

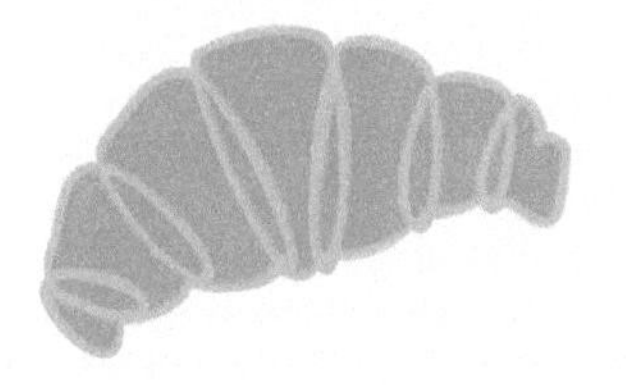

Croissant (krwah-sahn)

croissant

Céréale (seh-ree-yahl)

cereal

Oeuf (uhf)

egg

Yaourt (ya-oort)

yogurt

Jus d'orange (zhoo doh-ranzh)

orange juice

After breakfast, they all go for a walk. Delphine wonders what the surprise could be.

"Is it a new toy?" asks Delphine.

Jouets (zhoo-way)

Toys

Ballon (baa-law)

ball

Doudou (doo-doo)

stuffed animal

Cubes (koob)

blocks

Poupée (poo-pay)

doll

Chariot (shar-ee-yoh)

wagon

"Patience," says Maman.

"You'll have to wait and see."

"Am I getting new paints?"

Couleurs (coo-luhr)

Colors

Rouge (roozh)

red

Orange (oh-ranzh)

orange

Jaune (zhohn)

yellow

Vert (vehr)

green

Bleu (bluh)

blue

“Patience,” says Papa.

"You'll have to wait and see."

On their way home, they start to slow down.

Something catches Delphine's eye.

"Surprise, chérie!" says Maman.

"You start ballet classes tomorrow."

Delphine does a twirl and hugs her bunny.

It's better than anything she imagined.

La Danse Classique (la dahs claa-seek)

Ballet

Tendue (tahn-doo)

Passé (paa-say)

Demi plié (deh-mee plee-ay)

Relevé (reh-luh-vay)

Arabesque (a-ra-besk)

Later that night, Delphine smiles as she closes her eyes.

Today was a good day, and tomorrow will be even better.

Bon nuit.

Other Words We Learned

Maman (maa-mahn) – Mommy

Chien (shee-ah) – Dog

Bonjour (boh-zhoor) – Hello

Chérie (sheh-ree) – Dear

Bon nuit (boh-nwee) – Goodnight

ABOUT THE AUTHOR

Rita Tarnate is a native New Yorker currently residing in Denver with her husband, Alex, daughters, Odie and Charlie, and dog, Winter. She speaks six languages and loves exploring new places. This is her first picture book.

Learn more about her passion for traveling with little ones at www.hellozazu.com.

ABOUT THE ILLUSTRATOR

Leah Roides currently lives in Colorado with her wife Augusta and three fur babies, Wyatt, Zion, and Jack. Along with creating, she loves exploring the outdoors, traveling, photography and gardening.

CPSIA information can be obtained
at www.ICGtesting.com
Printed in the USA
LVHW071539200921
698272LV00009B/282

* 9 7 8 1 7 3 6 5 6 3 4 0 3 *